別貪心！斑斑貓！

Tabby Cat wants that!

Moira Butterfield 著

Rachael O'Neill 繪

Tabby Cat lives on Little Farm. She looks very soft and furry, but sometimes she is a very selfish cat who wants everything for herself.

斑斑貓住在小小農莊裡。她看起來毛又多又柔軟，但是有的時候呢，她會變得很自私，貪心地想擁有每一樣東西。

One day she sees Little Puppy chasing his toy ball in the farmyard. "I want that ball!" she says, and she takes it away from poor Little Puppy.

有一天，她看見小狗狗在院子裡追著玩具球玩耍，便說：「我要那顆球！」說完便把它從可憐的小狗狗手上搶走了。

Then Tabby Cat sees Little Lamb sleeping in a warm patch of sunlight. "I want to sit there!" says Tabby Cat, and she pushes Little Lamb out of the sun.

過了不久，斑斑貓看見羊咩咩舒服地睡在一片溫暖的陽光下。就對他說：「我要坐在這裡！」她便把羊咩咩擠到照不到陽光的地方。

Then Tabby Cat sees Little Pig wearing a smart red bow. "I want that!" says Tabby Cat, and she pulls the end of the bow until it falls off poor Little Pig.

接著，斑斑貓看到豬小弟戴著一個漂亮的紅色蝴蝶結。「我要那個蝴蝶結！」斑斑貓說完，便拉住蝴蝶結的尾端，把它從可憐的豬小弟身上扯了下來。

Tabby Cat finds the farmer's lunchbox. Inside there are lots of fishpaste sandwiches. "I want those!" thinks the greedy little cat, and she eats them all up.

斑斑貓發現了農夫的便當盒，裡頭有好多好多的魚醬三明治。「我要這些三明治！」貪心的小貓這樣想著，然後她就把全部的三明治都吃光了。

W hen the farmer comes back all his sandwiches are gone.
"I know who has eaten them!" he says angrily. "There are
cat's pawmarks all over my lunchbox!"

當農夫回來的時候，發現所有的三明治都被吃光
了。「我知道這是誰做的好事！」他生氣地說。「這飯
盒上全都是貓咪的腳印！」

The farmer sees Little Puppy looking sad. "Who took your ball?" he asks. He sees Little Lamb shivering with cold. "Who pushed you out of the sunshine?" he asks.

農夫看見小狗狗好像很難過的樣子，便問他：「是誰拿走了你的球呢？」農夫又看見羊咩咩冷得抖個不停，便問他：「是誰把你擠到沒有陽光的地方去的啊？」

The farmer finds Tabby Cat fast asleep in the sun. "We are going to teach you a lesson, you selfish little animal!" thinks the farmer to himself.

農夫發現斑斑貓躺在陽光下，睡得很香很甜，心裡想著：「我們一定要給你一個教訓才行，你這隻自私的小傢伙！」

When Tabby Cat wakes up she feels thirsty. She goes to the back door of the farmhouse to find her bowl of milk. But the bowl has disappeared!

斑斑貓睡醒後覺得很渴，於是她跑到屋子的後門去找她的牛奶碗。可是碗居然不見了！

The farmer has given the bowl to Little Lamb, and he has filled it up with cream. "That's not fair," shouts Tabby Cat angrily. "It belongs to me!"

原來，農夫把碗給了羊咩咩，還在裡頭倒滿了奶油。斑斑貓生氣地大吼著說：「不公平！這個碗是我的！」

Tabby Cat feels very hungry. She goes to the back door of the farmhouse to find her bowl of food. Oh dear, the food bowl has disappeared as well!

斑斑貓覺得很餓，於是她走到屋子的後門去找她的食物碗。哎呀！怎麼食物碗也不見了！

The farmer has given the food bowl to Little Pig. "That's MY food," shouts Tabby Cat angrily. "Give it back!" "Too late, I've eaten it!" says Little Pig.

原來，農夫已經把食物碗拿給豬小弟了。「那是我的食物吧！」斑斑貓很生氣地大叫。「把它還給我！」

Tabby Cat feels so angry that she doesn't want to speak to anyone. She creeps back to the farmhouse to sit on her cushion. Oh no, it has disappeared as well!

「太遲了啦！我已經把它吃光光了！」豬小弟說。斑斑貓很生氣，氣得不想和任何人講話。她慢慢地走回屋裡，想坐在她的墊子上。噢！不好了！連墊子也不見了！

The farmer has given the cushion to Little Puppy. He is chewing it, instead of sitting on it! "Give it back!" shouts Tabby Cat. "No, I like it!" says Little Puppy.

原來，農夫把墊子給了小狗狗。小狗狗正在啃它，而不是坐在上面。「把它還給我！」斑斑貓大聲叫著。「不要，我喜歡這個墊子嘛！」小狗狗說。

Tabby Cat feels very unhappy. All her favourite things have been given away to the other animals, and there is nothing she can do. "IT'S NOT FAIR!" she shouts.

斑斑貓覺得很不快樂。所有她喜歡的東西，都被分給其他的小動物了，而她卻又無可奈何。她大吼著說：「這真是太不公平了！」

"Oh yes it is," says the farmer. "I've treated you just like you treat your friends. Now you know what it's like to have your things taken away by a bully!"

「喔！不不不！這樣才公平！」農夫對她說。「我對待妳的方式，就像妳對待妳其他的朋友一樣。現在妳才知道，當妳的東西被惡霸搶走時，是什麼滋味了吧！」

"Oh dear, I don't want anyone else's things. I want my own!" cries Tabby Cat. "If I give back all the things I have taken, can I have my bowls and cushion back?"

「哎呀！我不想要別人的東西了啦！我只要我自己的嚕！」斑斑貓哭求著說。「如果我把拿來的東西都還回去，那我還能拿回我的碗和墊子嗎？」

"Hmm, all right," says the farmer. "I can see that you have learnt your lesson." He gives the milk bowl, the food bowl and the cushion back to Tabby Cat.

「嗯！好吧！」農夫說道。「我想妳已經得到教訓了。」於是，他便把牛奶碗、食物碗和墊子都還給了斑斑貓。

"Thank you!" says Tabby Cat. "I Want..." "Oh no. What do you want now?" cries the farmer. Tabby Cat looks up at him and smiles. "I want to say I'm sorry!" she says.

「謝謝你！」斑斑貓說。「我想要……」「噢！不好了！這下妳又要什麼東西啦？」農夫無可奈何地說。斑斑貓抬頭看了看農夫並笑著說：「我只是想說聲對不起啦！」